PRINCESS TALES
AROUND THE WORLD

ONCE UPON A TIME IN RHYME WITH SEEK-AND-FIND PICTURES

ADAPTED BY
GRACE MACCARONE

ILLUSTRATED BY
GAIL DE MARCKEN

FEIWEL AND FRIENDS • NEW YORK

SEEK AND FIND

EXPLORE THE WORLD OF ONCE UPON A TIME.

Read the stories. Then pore over pictures filled with treasures and trinkets. And join the quest to find hidden objects in the list that accompanies each illustration. After you're done, explore some more. In every picture, look for an apple, ballet slippers, a blue bracelet, blue and white stripes, blue silk fabric with red butterflies, a book, a pair of glasses, a rabbit, a red wig, a snake, and a star. Good luck!

Table of Contents

RAPUNZEL

A woman, soon to be a mother,
desired rampion, nothing other.
"Get me some or I will die,"
she said. Her husband said he'd try.
It grew within a witch's wall.
And though this witch was feared by all,
the faithful husband risked his life
and stole the rampion for his wife.
The witch appeared without delay.
"That's mine!" she shouted. "You must pay!"
The man agreed. The witch just smiled.
"When it's born, I'll take your child."
The child was born. The witch soon came.
She said, "Rapunzel is your name."
The girl was lovely to behold,
with yards of hair of rosy gold.
But when the child was twelve years old,
the witch employed her dreadful power
to build a stairless, doorless tower.
She kept Rapunzel trapped in there.
"Rapunzel, dear, let down your hair,"
announced the witch, and every day,
she'd climb the copper locks and stay
a little while, then go away.
A prince was riding through a wood

and came to where the tower stood.
And while the prince meandered there,
such lovely singing filled the air.
So potent was Rapunzel's art,
her song transformed the prince's heart.
He searched for gate or hatch or door.
A distant window. Nothing more.
That night the prince lay in his bed;
Rapunzel's voice besieged his head.
The prince, aware he had no choice,
returned at dawn to hear the voice.
The witch arrived but didn't see
the lovesick prince behind a tree.
"Rapunzel, dear, let down your hair,"
she said, and tresses filled the air.
The witch ascended unaware
an ardent prince was watching there.
That evening at the seventh hour,
the steadfast prince approached the tower.
Standing near the massive wall,
the prince reprised the witch's call.
"Rapunzel, dear, let down your hair,"
and down came yards of locks most fair.
The prince took hold and didn't stop
until he reached the very top.

Find Little Red Riding Hood and the Wolf, a violin,
6 golden doves, 3 nestlings, and a mustache.

At first, the girl was filled with fright
to see a stranger come by night.
But as the prince's heart was true,
Rapunzel's love awakened, too.
The prince asked, "Will you marry me?"
Rapunzel answered, "Happily.
Bring fifty skeins of silk to weave
a ladder so that I may leave."
Eager for Rapunzel's flight,
the prince delivered one each night.
The witch was clueless, but one day,
Rapunzel gave herself away.
"Tell me, Dame, why of the two,
the prince is sprightlier than you?"
Hearing this, the witch went wild.
"I'll punish you, you wicked child!"
She cut Rapunzel's lovely hair

and took her to a desert where
Rapunzel grieved from hour to hour.
The prince, returning to the tower,
climbed the copper mane to see
a witch and not his bride-to-be.
The prince leapt from Rapunzel's tower
and landed in a thorny bower.
And though he lived, the prince was blind.
He roamed the forest, wept, and pined
until one day, he heard a sound
so sweet and pure, he knew he'd found
his bride, who cried to see his plight.
And True Love's tears restored his sight.
The prince's kingdom wasn't far.
So there they went, and there they are.

Find the Giant and the Beanstalk, a harp,
6 lizards, and a pair of scissors.

THE GOLDEN GOOSE

A wife and husband had two sons.
Their favorite was the older one.
His mother gave him cake and tea
and sent him off to chop a tree.
In the wood, his work began,
when "Please," announced a frail old man.
"I'm hungry and I'm thirsty, too.
May I share your snack with you?"
The youth said, "No! It's just for me,"
but when he tried to cut the tree,
he missed and cut himself instead.
The old man grinned and shook his head.

The youth went home, his greed to blame.
His task undone and feeling shame,
the older brother hid in bed.
The younger brother, Dummling, said,
"I'd like to try to cut wood, too."
"Your brother failed and so will you,"
his mother and his father said.
With water and with day-old bread,
to the forest Dummling ran.
Arriving quickly, he began,
when "Please," announced a frail old man.
"I'm thirsty and I'm hungry, too.

May I share your snack with you?"
"Of course," the kindly Dummling said.
"It's water and it's day-old bread."
But when the lad withdrew his bread,
the bread had turned to cake instead.
And so, the water turned to tea.
The man and lad ate heartily.
"Because you're kind and shared your snack,
I would like to pay you back,"
the old man said. "Now, chop that tree,
and at the bottom you will see
something that will change your life,
will bring you riches and a wife!"
The lad obeyed and cut the spruce,

and at its roots, a golden goose!
Dummling took it to an inn.
The landlord's daughters sat within.
A tired Dummling fell asleep.
The girls approached, without a peep.
The eldest daughter tried to pluck
a feather from the goose. She stuck!
And when the second daughter tried,
her hand stuck to her sister's side.
And though they tried to warn the last,
ignoring them, she, too, stuck fast.
The golden goose, a magic glue,
attached the sisters all night through.
When Dummling woke at break of day,

he grabbed the goose and ran away.
Dummling didn't seem to mind
the landlord's daughters trailed behind.
But when a parson came along,
he thought the girls were doing wrong.
The parson didn't understand.
He caught the youngest by the hand.
"It isn't proper to pursue
that man," he lectured. "Shame on you."
But then the parson fastened, too.
Two workers rushed to give some aid
but failed and joined the strange parade.
The goose and all her following
approached a city where a king

had great concern about his child,
who never laughed and never smiled.
"To any man who makes her laugh,"
the king proclaimed, "I'll give him half
of what I earn from all my land,
and furthermore, my daughter's hand.
The goose parade went stumbling past.
The princess cracked a smile at last,
exploded into full-blown laughter.
She and Dummling wed soon after.
Dummling's friend withdrew the spell,
and all were freed. Now all is well.

Find Ferdinand the Bull, a guitar, 2 babies in slings,
a pair of green sandals, and a rope belt.

THE LITTLE MERMAID

The loveliest voice that ever shall be
belonged to a princess who lived in the sea.
Within the ocean, way down deep,
this little mermaid was asleep.
Her sisters came with shakes and pokes.
With blinks and yawns, the mermaid woke.
The mermaids raced to castle halls
and sang all day in coral walls.
At age fifteen, the culmination
of each mermaid's education:
all alone, the girl would rise
to see the land with her own eyes.
Now fifteen carefree years had passed.
The youngest's turn had come at last.
Adorned with seashells in her hair,
the girl emerged to greet the air.
The wind was calm, and on the sea,
a regal ship sat tranquilly.
Through cabin holes, the girl surveyed;
people danced while music played,
when someone took her by surprise—
a prince with soulful, coal-black eyes.
The smitten girl could not ignore
she was in love, no less, no more.
Suddenly, the waves grew high.
Heavy storm clouds filled the sky.
The ocean moaned, the ocean lashed;
the doomed ship groaned as lightning flashed.
Water rushed and broke the mast.
The noble ship was sinking fast.
The prince was swallowed by the water.
Seeing this, the sea king's daughter
swam swiftly to the prince's side.
The prince, unconscious, could have died.

Find Pinocchio and the Whale, a lyre, a swordfish,
a red sea urchin, and a pink sea horse.

They drifted slowly till they reached
the safety of a sandy beach.
And as the night turned into day,
she kissed his head and swam away.
A young girl, walking by the bay,
came to where the prince now lay.
In time, some other folks arrived.
The lucky prince was soon revived.
The mermaid left the prince behind
but could not get him off her mind.
She asked the whales to find out where
his castle stood and sought him there
and watched him sail around the bay.
The mermaid's love increased each day.
She resolved to make a switch.
So, off she went to find the witch.
She swam past creatures cruel and dreaded:
wormy fingered, serpent headed.
"I'll give you legs," the sea witch said,
"but if your prince decides to wed
another girl, then you will die.
And one more thing, my cutie pie.
For my price, I'll take your voice."
The mermaid said, "I have no choice."
The mermaid traveled through the ocean,
in her hands the magic potion.
Arriving at the palace shore,
she drank the draught. Forevermore,
her tail was gone, and as she rose,
she felt her legs and feet and toes
in such great pain, she fainted there.
Waking to the prince's stare,
she wrapped her body in her hair.
The prince inquired, "Who are you?"
Without her voice, the mermaid knew
there was little she could do
but pray that he would recognize

the love she spoke of with her eyes.
She never left the prince's side—
every day, they'd walk and ride.
And then one day, his parents planned
to send him to a foreign land
to meet a lovely princess there
and fall in love and have an heir.
Carried by a stately ship,
the prince and mermaid made the trip.
They met the princess of the land,
who smiled and took the prince's hand.
"Enchanted," said the prince, surprised
to see a girl he recognized,
to see a girl he saw before,
the girl who found him on the shore.
Thinking she had saved his life,
he asked the girl to be his wife.
The mermaid girl was devastated.
She lost her prince; her death awaited.
But, no! Misfortune was abated!
She gazed beyond the harbor where
her sisters waved . . . without their hair!
Suddenly, the sea king's daughter
fled and dived into the water.
The mermaid was ecstatic when
her legs became a tail again.
The witnesses saw only foam,
but we all know the girl swam home,
surrounded by her sisters, who
had visited the sea witch, too.
They gave the sea witch what she prized
to save their sister from demise.
Our mermaid never sang again,
but she was happy in the end.

Find Peter Pan, Tinker Bell, Captain Hook
and the Crocodile, a gourd clarinet, 3 chameleons,
and a kraken.

THE FIREBIRD

Prince Ivan, hunting late one day,
pursued a stag and lost his way.
He saw a castle, dark and grim.
Its magic seemed to beckon him.
In a palace garden, he
beheld a golden apple tree.
Sensing he was not alone,
he saw a band of knights in stone.
A dazzling bird made bright the sky,
then settled on the ground nearby.
From where he hid, the prince could see

the bird pick apples from the tree.
Frozen there, as in a trance,
he watched the stunning creature dance.
And then, the prince perceived his chance.
Springing forth, Prince Ivan wrapped
his arms around her. She was trapped!
She tried to flail; she tried to flee.
The prince withstood tenaciously.
She quailed and quaked pathetically;
he felt regret and set her free.
As he released her from her tether,
she gave the prince a splendid feather
to summon her. In time of need,

she'd go to him and intercede.
The bird flew off to find her nest;
the prince lay down to take a rest.
Just before the break of day,
twelve princesses came out to play.
Tossing apples in the air,
the maidens soon became aware
a handsome prince was standing there.
The prince came forth to join the game.
A girl—Tatiana was her name—
urged the prince to go away.
"You must depart without delay.
Though now we play among the flowers,

an evil king with magic powers
captured us and cast a spell,
and on the knights, now stone as well."
The love-struck prince became entranced
as twelve young maidens sang and danced,
then left him once again alone
among the hapless knights of stone.
Prince Ivan didn't hesitate
to open up the castle gate.
In a flash, alarms released
every ilk of wicked beast—
with bark and bite and brawn and sting—
followed by their evil king.

The king announced, "Unwelcome guest,
I'll make you stone, just like the rest."
Before the king could cast his spell,
the prince withdrew from his lapel
the magic feather, like a flame.
The firebird, as promised, came.
She cast a spell upon the king
and beasts to make them sway and swing.
They kicked and squatted, jumped and hopped.
The creatures danced until they dropped.
She meanwhile took the prince to see
a giant egg atop a tree.
To get the egg, the prince climbed high.

He boldly held it to the sky.
The king, revived, was horrified.
That egg concealed his soul inside.
The egg was smashed; the bad king died.
The granite knights changed back to men,
the princesses were free again,
the king's repulsive creatures fled.
Tatiana and Prince Ivan wed.
The Firebird flew overhead.

Find Peter and the Wolf, the cat, the bluebird,
the duck, the fox, 6 bells, a pink-striped dress,
and a golden egg.

SCHEHERAZADE

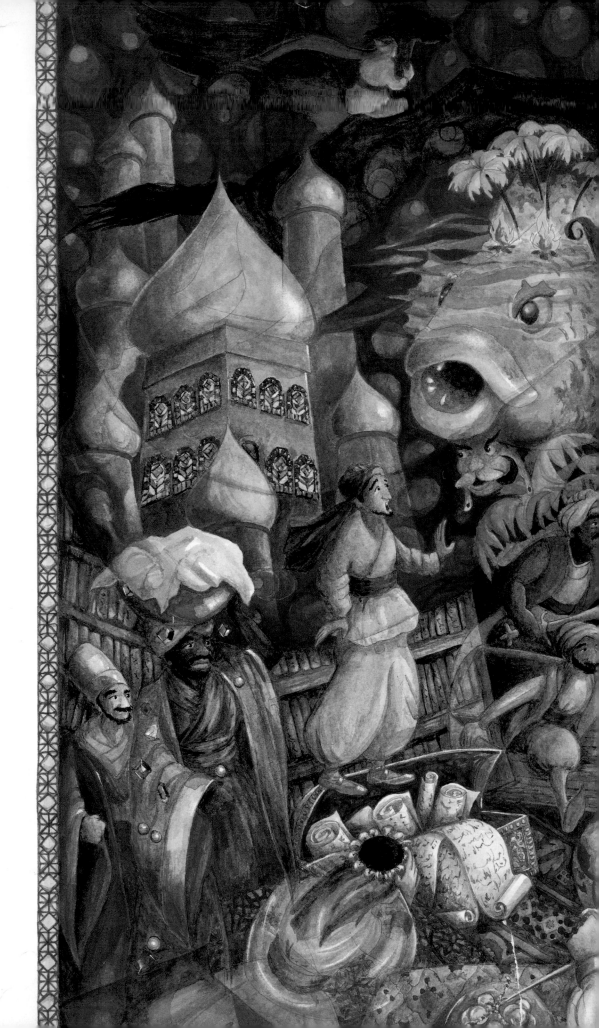

Scheherazade woke up and looked
around at all her precious books:
history, science, math, and art
and poems that she'd learned by heart.
She lived with the vizier, her dad,
who served the king—once good, now bad.
The king, forsaken by his wife,
became enraged and took her life,
then married someone new each night
and had her killed by morning's light.
Scheherazade was brave and good.
She'd stop the killing if she could.
"I'm marrying the king," she said.
The grand-vizier was filled with dread.
The king was overjoyed to wed
a girl both pretty and well-read.
So when his bride began to cry,
the king saw fit to ask her why.
"I have a sister, sire, whom I
would like to see before I die,"
a sly Scheherazade replied.
The sister soon was at her side.
As planned, the sister would prevail
upon the king to hear a tale.
Scheherazade would then recite
a story that endured all night.
But just before the story ended—
as Scheherazade intended—
at dawn, the king was called away.
He let her live another day!
And so, it went from night to night:
a story stopping at its height.
A thousand stories saved her life.
By now, the king adored his wife,
released her from her execution,
and all were pleased with that solution.

Find the Three Little Pigs and the Wolf, a lute,
a scimitar, a ship, 2 candles, and 3 gold shoes.

PRINCESS MOONLIGHT

A bamboo cutter and his wife
were poor and childless, late in life.
The husband, cutting stalks one day,
came across a rare display:
a tiny girl upon a leaf
and casting light beyond belief.
The husband didn't hesitate.
He saw the child and knew his fate.
The couple loved her as their own.
In several days, the girl had grown
to reach an average human height,

but never did she lose her light.
A glow projected through her skin,
revealing goodness from within.
And that's why Princess Moonlight came
to be the cherished orphan's name.
Her father now would cut bamboo
and find a piece of gold or two.
The family soon was well-to-do.
And every day, the daughter grew
more lovely; thus, throughout the land,
suitors vied to win her hand.

The girl tenaciously resisted;
five princes stubbornly persisted.
Because she didn't wish to wed,
their visits filled the girl with dread.
The princess figured out a way
to make her suitors go away.
She gave each prince a marriage test
and sent him on a futile quest:
the Buddha's bowl; the Fire Rat's coat;
a ruby from a dragon's throat;
branches from the golden tree;
a snail shell found, not in the sea,
but laid inside a swallow's nest.

The princes failed, although they tried.
They brought her fakes and boldly lied.
Their tricks exposed, the girl replied
she would not be a cheater's bride.
Accused, the men departed fast.
The princess found some peace at last.
So great was Princess Moonlight's fame,
one day, the emperor also came.
He loved the girl, but in the end,
he was content to be her friend.
Now the winter turned to spring.
Something odd was happening.
She'd see the moon and start to cry.

In time, she told her parents why.
"I am a princess from the moon.
A ship will come to get me soon."
The princess was profoundly sad
to leave the earthly life she had,
to leave her parents, whom she loved,
and face uncertainty above.
The emperor sent two thousand guards,
who filled her house and fields and yards.
A glowing ship arrived at night;
the guards were blinded by its light.
The princess, though, had come to see
the moon would be her destiny.

She kissed her mom and dad good-bye
and made a voyage through the sky.
Her parents missed her, so they'd climb
the highest hill from time to time.
At the top, they burned a note,
content to watch the ashes float.
They sent their love in smoke up high;
she sent them moonbeams in reply.

*Find the Tortoise and the Hare, a flute, 4 butterflies,
a snail, a sword, and a tiny princess.*

THE PRINCESS ON THE GLASS HILL

A farmer had a field of hay
that disappeared one St. John's Day.
The hay was gone the next year, too.
The man's frustration grew and grew.
The farmer, at year three, assigned
his oldest son the task to mind
the hayfield. Said the oldest son,
"Count on me. It will be done!"
On St. John's Eve, he tried to doze
inside the hut; a racket rose.
The roof above began to shake.
The earth below began to quake.
The oldest brother ran away.
The hay was gone on St. John's Day.
The farmer, at year four, assigned
his second son the task to mind
the field. The second tried to doze
inside the hut; a racket rose.
The second brother ran away.
The hay was gone on St. John's Day.
The hapless farmer had three sons
but much preferred the older ones.
The youngest had a sooty face
from living by the fireplace.
With flint and steel, young Boots would sit
and make the fire and keep it lit.
Year five, the youngest son—although
his brothers laughed—prepared to go.

They ridiculed, but Boots held fast.
He knew his chance had come at last.
On St. John's Eve, he tried to doze
inside the hut; a racket rose.
The roof above began to shake.
The earth below began to quake.
Boots surmised, "I'm still okay.
It could be worse, so I will stay."
The racket grew; the earth shook more.
Boots bounced and tumbled to the floor.
He said again, "I'm still okay.
It could be worse, so I will stay."
The biggest earthquake came and then
all was peaceful once again.
Boots tried to sleep but heard a sound.
He took a look outside and found
a stallion grazing on the grass
and gleaming armor made of brass.
Boots tossed his steel upon the horse.
Its magic tamed the steed, of course.
He hid the horse and armor, too,
and ran to see his brothers, who,
when they looked at break of day,
saw the meadow filled with hay.

Find the Little Red Hen, the cat, the duck, the pig,
a horn, a pink flag, and a bonfire.

Boots' brothers spurned Boots anyway
and shared the gossip of the day:
the king announced, throughout the land,
a contest for his daughter's hand.
The girl would sit atop a hill
and hold a golden apple till
a man on horseback reached her, then
he'd take the apple down again.
There was a hitch—the hill was glass;
the test impossible to pass.
Princes came from far and wide;
each sought the princess as his bride.
But every noble steed that tried
to climb the hill would slip and slide,
until a dashing knight in brass
rode partway up the hill of glass.
The princess tossed the apple; when
he caught it, he went down again.
The crowd of people watching cheered.
The knight rode off. He disappeared.
To find the knight, a search began.
The king examined every man—
nobles, peasants, Boots' two brothers—
and asked if there were any others.
The king discovered only one:
a much disparaged youngest son.
Boots held the apple in his hand
and claimed his bride and half the land.

Find 7 ravens, a ghost, a horn, a purple flag,
a hut, and 4 flower crowns.

THE LOATHSOME DRAGON

Princess Margaret and her brother
had a father but no mother.
Her brother, Wynde,* an unproved knight,
had traveled far away to fight.
The girl was waiting for the king
who'd traveled, too, and soon would bring
a handsome woman, his new bride,
elegant but full of pride.
Princess Margaret aimed to please.
She gave the queen a ring of keys.
"These keys are for the palace doors,"
the princess said. "Now all is yours."
A lord, in earshot of the queen,
remarked that he had never seen,
in all the world, a maiden fair
as Princess Margaret standing there.
Enraged, the queen, a witch, then cast
a spell: "Her beauty will not last."
The girl became a dragon and,
breathing fire, destroyed the land.
For seven miles, both to and fro,
no blade of grass or corn could grow.
When Wynde learned of the devastation
that befell his cherished nation,
he built a ship and went to sea;
Wynde met the dragon presently.

But as he drew his sword to fight,
he heard his sister's voice recite:

*"Oh, quit thy sword, unbend thy bow,
and give me kisses three.
For though I seem a dragon,
no harm I'll do to thee."*

On hearing Princess Margaret's voice,
Childe Wynde knew he had no choice.
He kissed the dragon, as it said,
and when he did, the dragon shed
its horns and wings and armored skin,
revealing Margaret from within.
But brother Wynde knew magic, too.
Before the queen could start to do
more harm, Wynde changed her to a toad.
Now she hops along the road
and spits on maids who pass her way,
a vengeful creature to this day.

*Wynde rhymes with kind.

*Find Puss in Boots,
bagpipes, a red brooch,
11 swords, and a toad.*

25

TOADS AND DIAMONDS

Two sisters, nothing like each other,
lived together with their mother.
The elder was unkind and cold.
The younger had a heart of gold.
Twice a day, the younger daughter
walked three miles to fetch their water.
"I'd like some water from your pail,"
said a woman, old and frail.
The girl put water in a cup.
The older woman drank it up.
"Because you're mannerly and pleasant,"
said the woman, "here's a present.
For every word you utter, you'll
expel a flower or a jewel."

(The woman, you should realize,
in truth's a fairy in disguise.)
Home later than anticipated,
the girl found Mother irritated.
"You took too long," she reprimanded.
"What's your reason?" she demanded.
"I beg your pardon," said the girl,
and with her words released a pearl,
a jade, one flower, then another.
"What is this?" inquired her mother.
In great detail, the girl explained
while roses, mums, and rubies rained.
The mother sent her elder daughter
to serve the same old woman water.

The daughter told her mother no.
Her mother answered, "You must go!"
The elder daughter did as told
in search of someone frail and old
but found a lady, nicely dressed,
approaching with the same request.
"I'd like some water from your pail,"
said the lady, young and hale.
The daughter said, "It's not for you."
The lady was the fairy, too!
"Because you're selfish and unpleasant,"
said the fairy, "here's a present.
For every word or sound you make,
you'll spew a toad or newt or snake."
The girl rushed home. Her mom said, "Well?"
"Well," said the girl. A vine snake fell.

The mother blamed her younger child,
hurled cups and plates and acted wild.
The girl ran quickly as she could,
not stopping till she reached a wood.
The maiden soon became aware
a handsome king was hunting there.
He asked the maiden why she cried.
A diamond issued when she sighed.
Delivering her explanation,
she won the monarch's adoration.
Producing gems for her own ring,
the younger daughter wed a king.
Detesting vermin all around,
the elder lived without a sound.

*Find Mowgli, Bagheera and Shere Khan, a gong,
a red gem, and 2 yellow roses.*

27

Six Swans

A king, whose cherished wife had died,
remarried. Fearing his new bride
would harm his heirs, he had them hide.
An isolated castle stood
protected by a pathless wood.
There the monarch's children stayed;
there they slept and worked and played.
A hearty girl and six bold boys
infused the wood with joyful noise.
A wise old woman gave the king
a giant ball of magic string.
This ball of string would self-unwind
and lead the king to where he'd find
his girl and boys. He watched them grow.
The queen decided she must know
exactly where the king would go.
She bribed the servants who revealed
the secret that the king concealed.
She planned to do the children harm;
she sewed silk shirts that held a charm.
She found the string that led the way
and saw six boys outside at play.
She quickly tossed the shirts upon
their backs, and each became a swan.
With wings and feathers, off they flew.
The evil queen departed, too,
not knowing that a girl inside
was watching and was horrified.
The princess ran away to seek
her brothers, now in bird physique.
She walked and walked without a stop
through densest woods; she thought she'd drop.
And as the day turned into night,

she witnessed six wild swans alight,
shed their down and feathers, then
reclaim her brothers' forms again.
She crept out from a hiding place
to give each boy a warm embrace.
The brothers, quelling her delight,
explained they'd soon resume their flight.
"For fifteen minutes, we can shed
our birdlike traits," a brother said.
She pleaded, "Brothers, please do tell
what I may do to break the spell."
"To break the spell, on our behalf,
you may not say a word or laugh
for six full years in which you sew
six starwort shirts that you must throw
upon our backs," she heard them say
as they transformed and flew away.
Seated in a willow tree,
she started work immediately.
A prince and huntsman passing by
saw her there and wondered why.
They called to her from on the ground.
The princess didn't make a sound.
The prince and huntsman took her down
and brought the princess into town.
Entering the castle walls,
they settled into splendid halls.
The princess dressed in satin gowns,
with golden rings and diamond crowns.
She kept on sewing, always mum;
yet the prince was overcome.
Acknowledging that he'd prefer
this silent girl, he married her.

Find the Ugly Duckling, a post horn,
a sewing needle, a small creek, and a bow.

The prince's mother, curious
about the girl and furious
about the marriage, did her best
to put the princess to the test.
When the couple had an heir,
the prince's mother, then and there,
hid the couple's child and said,
"The princess killed her son! He's dead!"
Unable to expose the lie,
the princess was condemned to die.
Determined that she wouldn't fail,
the loyal sister sewed in jail.
About six years elapsed by now.
With five shirts done, she'd kept her vow.
The sixth shirt needed one more sleeve.
The princess, though, was forced to leave
her cell and, facing death by fire,
courageously approached the pyre.
Her eyes were focused on the sky,
where six wild swans were flying by.
She tossed the shirts upon them; then,
the six wild swans became young men.
Though one maintained a feathered wing,
he felt it was a minor thing.
With satisfaction unsurpassed,
the silent princess spoke at last.
"I didn't kill my son," she said.
"I know my baby is not dead."
The boy was found and reunited
with his mother, much excited.
She persevered, and wrongs were righted.

*Find the Nutcracker, Marie, the Mouse King,
an accordion, 8 torches, a fishing pole, and a
child picking flowers.*